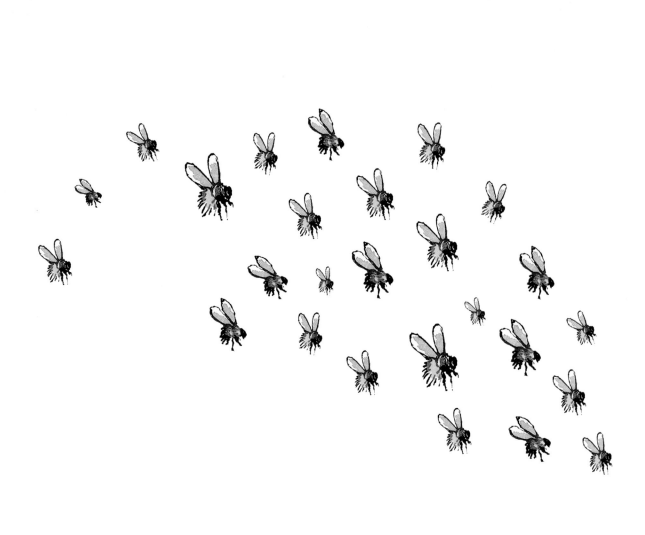

# Winnie-the-Pooh
# Story Treasury

DEAN

"I wish to pay tribute to the work of E.H. Shepard
which has been inspirational in the creation
of these new drawings."
*Andrew Grey*

# EGMONT
*We bring stories to life*

First published in Great Britain 2003.
This edition reissued 2013 by Dean, an imprint of Egmont UK Limited
The Yellow Building, 1 Nicholas Road, London W11 4AN
Illustrations by Andrew Grey
Based on the "Winnie-the-Pooh" works
by A. A. Milne and E.H. Shepard
Text © The Trustees of the Pooh Properties
Illustrations © 2013 Disney Enterprises, Inc.

ISBN 978 0 6035 6798 8
53985/1
Printed in China

# Contents

# This book belongs to:

...............................................

# These stories take place

NICE FOR PIKNICKS

P
O — O
H

SANDY PIT
WHERE ROO PLAYS

KANGAS
HOUSE

POOH BEARS
HOUSE

RABBITS
HOUSE

SIX PINE TREES

POOH tRAP FOR
HEFFALUMPS

PIGLETS
HOUSE

WHERE
THE WOOZLE
WASNT

FLOODY PLACE

Kanga

Winnie-the-Pooh

Owl

Piglet

Roo

# Characters

Christopher
Robin

Eeyore

Rabbit      Tigger

# A Poem about Pooh

Pooh is a Silly Old Bear
Who lives life without a care.
He's happiest when he has honey,
The taste of it makes him go funny,
Goloptious honey, sticky and runny!

That clever Bear of Little Brain,
Saved Piglet from the pouring rain!
There's nothing that he wouldn't do,
Life is fun with friends like you.

The Best Bear in All the World - Pooh!

# A Poem about Eeyore

Eeyore is old, he's grey and he's slow,
He may, if you're lucky, nod a hello,
But he's probably pondering a sad reflection
And thinking with gloom of his sorry dejection.

Eeyore eats thistles, and wonders "Why?"
He may, if you're lucky, look up with a sigh,
But mostly his low expectations are such
That he's grateful to any who think of him much.

# A Poem about Tigger

He came to the Forest late one night,
The noise was enough to give Pooh a fright.
"Worraworraworra," he said,
And Pooh got out of bed,
To find a Bouncy Tigger ahead.

Tigger now lives with Kanga and Roo,
Eating enough Medicine for two!
Never was an animal bouncier than he,
(Except when he was stuck up a tree.)

A Friendlier Tigger there never will be!

# A Poem about Piglet

Piglet is Small
But that's not all:
His bravery shows
That when the wind blows
His dear friends mean more than ever before
As he battles his way through a bluster.

So what does he do?
With persuasion from Pooh,
He climbs up some string
(What a Very Grand Thing),
To go and fetch help (not so much as a yelp)
And save his dear friends from a fluster.

# Pooh Goes Visiting

Winnie-the-Pooh was walking through the Forest, humming proudly to himself. He had made up a little hum as he was doing his Stoutness Exercises in front of the glass:

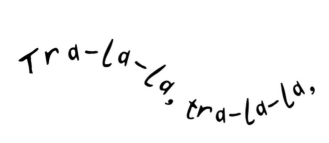

as he stretched up as high as he could go, and then

as he tried to reach his toes.

After breakfast he had learnt it off by heart, and now he
was humming it right through properly. It went like this:

Tra-la-la tra-la-la,

Tra-la-la, tra-la-la,

Rum-tum-tiddle-um-tum.

Tiddle-iddle tiddle-iddle,

Tiddle-iddle, tiddle-iddle,

Rum-tum-tum-tiddle-um.

Pooh was humming this hum to himself, when suddenly he came to a sandy bank, and in the bank was a large hole. "Aha!" said Pooh. (Rum-tum-tiddle-um-tum.) "If I know anything about anything, that hole means Rabbit and Rabbit means Company, and Company means Food and such like. Rum-tum-tum-tiddle-um."

So he bent down, put his head into the hole, and called out: "Is anybody at home?"

There was a sudden scuffling noise from inside the hole, and then silence.

"What I said was, 'Is anybody at home?'" called out Pooh very loudly.

"No!" said a voice; and then added, "You needn't shout, I heard you quite well the first time."

"Bother!" said Pooh. "Isn't there anybody here at all?"

"Nobody."

27

Pooh thought to himself, "There must be somebody there, because **somebody** must have said 'Nobody.'"

So he put his head back in the hole, and said:

"Well, could you very kindly tell me where Rabbit is?"

"He has gone to see his friend Pooh Bear," said Rabbit.

"But this is **Me!**" said Pooh, very much surprised.

"Are you sure?" said Rabbit, still more surprised.

"Quite, quite sure," said Pooh.

"Oh, well then, come in."

So Pooh pushed

and pushed and pushed

his way through the hole, and at last he got in.

"You were quite right," said Rabbit, looking at him all over.

"It is you. Glad to see you."

"Who did you think it was?"

"Well, I wasn't sure. You know how it is in the Forest.

One can't have anybody coming into one's house. One has

to be careful. What about a mouthful of *something*?"

Pooh **always** liked a little *something* at eleven o'clock in the morning, and he was very glad to see Rabbit getting out the plates and mugs. When Rabbit said, "Honey or condensed milk with your bread?" he was so excited that he said, "Both," and then, so as not to seem greedy, he added, "But don't bother about the bread, please." And for a long time after that he said nothing.

At last, humming to himself in a rather sticky voice, Pooh got up, shook Rabbit lovingly by the paw, and said that he must be going on.

"Must you?" said Rabbit politely.

"Well," said Pooh, "I could stay a little longer if it – if you –" and he tried very hard to look in the direction of the larder.

"As a matter of fact," said Rabbit, "I was going out myself directly."

"Oh well, then, I'll be going on. Goodbye."

"Well, goodbye, if you're sure you won't have any more."

"Is there any more?" asked Pooh quickly.

Rabbit took the covers off the dishes and said, "No, there isn't."

"I thought not," said Pooh, nodding to himself.

"Well, goodbye. I must be going on."

So he started to climb out of the hole.

He **pulled** with his front paws,

and **pushed** with his back paws,

and in a little while his nose was

out in the open again . . . and

then his ears . . . and then his

front paws . . . and then his

shoulders . . . and then –

"Oh, help!" said Pooh.

"I'd better go back."

"Oh, bother!" said Pooh.

"I shall have to go on."

"I can't do either!" said Pooh.

"Oh, help and bother!"

Now, by this time Rabbit wanted
to go for a walk too, and finding the
front door **full**, he went out by
the back door, and came
round to Pooh, and
looked at him.

"Hallo, are you stuck?" he asked.

"N-no," said Pooh carelessly. "Just resting and thinking and humming to myself."

"Here, give us a paw," said Rabbit.

Pooh Bear stretched out a paw, and Rabbit pulled and pulled and pulled . . .

"Ow!" cried Pooh. "You're hurting!"

"The fact is," said Rabbit, "you're stuck."

"It all comes," said Pooh crossly, "of not having front doors big enough."

"It all comes," said Rabbit sternly, "of eating too much. Well, well, I shall go and fetch Christopher Robin."

Christopher Robin lived at the other end of the Forest. When he came back with Rabbit, and saw the front half of Pooh sticking out of the hole, he said, "Silly old Bear," in such a loving voice that everybody felt quite hopeful again.

"I was just beginning to think," said Pooh, sniffing slightly, "that Rabbit might never be able to use his front door again. And I should hate that," he said.

"So should I," said Rabbit.

"Of course he'll use his front door again," said Christopher Robin.

"Good," said Rabbit.

"If we can't pull you out, Pooh, we might push you back."

Rabbit scratched his whiskers thoughtfully, and pointed out that when Pooh was pushed back, he was back –

"You mean **I'd never get out?**" said Pooh.

"I mean," said Rabbit, "that having got so far, it seems a pity to waste it."

Christopher Robin nodded.

"Then there's only one thing to be done," he said.

"We shall have to wait for you to get thin again."

"How long does **getting thin take?**" asked Pooh anxiously.

"About a week, I should think," said Christopher Robin.

"But I can't stay here for a week!"

"You can stay here all right, **silly old Bear.** It's getting you **out** which is so difficult."

"We'll read to you," said Rabbit cheerfully. "And I say, you're taking up a good deal of room in my house – do you mind if I use your back legs as a towel-rail? Because, I mean, there they are – doing nothing – and it would be very convenient just to hang the towels on them."

"A week!" said Pooh gloomily. "What about meals?"

"I'm afraid no meals," said Christopher Robin, "because of getting thin quicker. But we will read to you."

Pooh began to sigh, and then found he couldn't because he was so **tightly stuck**; and a tear rolled down his eye as he said: "Then would you read a Sustaining Book, such as would help and comfort a Wedged Bear in Great Tightness?" So for a week Christopher Robin read that sort of book at the North end of Pooh,

and Rabbit hung his washing on the South end . . .
and in between, Pooh felt himself getting slenderer
and slenderer.

Then at the end of the week Christopher Robin said, "Now!" And he took hold of Pooh's front paws while

Rabbit took hold of Christopher Robin,

and all Rabbit's friends and relations

took hold of Rabbit, and they

all pulled together. . .

And for a long time Pooh

only said "Ow!"

And "Oh!"

And then, all of a sudden, he said:

"POP!"

just as if a cork

were coming out of a bottle.

And Christopher Robin and Rabbit and all

Rabbit's friends and relations went **head-over-heels**

**backwards** . . . and on the top of them came

Winnie-the-Pooh – free.

46

So, with a nod of thanks to his friends, he went on with his walk through the forest, humming proudly to himself. Christopher Robin looked after him lovingly, and said to himself, "Silly old Bear!"

# The End

# Tigger is Unbounced

One hot summer's day, Rabbit was talking to Pooh and Piglet. Pooh wasn't really listening. From time to time, he opened his eyes to say "Ah!"

Rabbit said, "You see what I mean, Piglet," and Piglet nodded to show that he did.

"In fact," said Rabbit, "Tigger's getting so Bouncy nowadays that it's time we taught him a lesson. Don't you think so, Piglet?"

Piglet agreed Tigger was very Bouncy and if they

could think of a way of unbouncing him, it would be

a Very Good Idea.

"What do *you* say, Pooh?" asked Rabbit.

Pooh opened his eyes and said, "Extremely."

"Extremely what?" asked Rabbit.

"What you were saying," said Pooh. "Undoubtably."

"But how shall we do it?" asked Piglet. "What sort of a lesson?"

"That's the point," said Rabbit.

"What were we talking about?" asked Pooh.

Piglet explained they were trying to think of a way to get the **bounces** out of Tigger, because however much you **liked** him, you couldn't deny it, he **did bounce**.

"Oh, I see," said Pooh. He tried to think, but he could only think of something which **didn't help at all**.

So he hummed it very quietly to himself.

If Rabbit
Was bigger
And fatter
And stronger,

or bigger
Than Tigger,

If Tigger was smaller,

Then Tigger's bad habit
of bouncing at Rabbit

Would matter
No longer,
If Rabbit was taller.

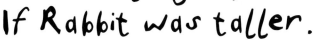

"I've an idea!" said Rabbit. "We take Tigger for a long explore and we lose him. The next morning we find him again and he'll be a **different Tigger** altogether. He'll be a **Humble** Tigger,

a Sad Tigger,

a Melancholy Tigger,

a Small and Sorry Tigger,

an *Oh-Rabbit-I-am-glad-to-see-you* Tigger.

That's why."

"I should hate him to go on being Sad," said Piglet.

"Tiggers never go on being Sad," explained Rabbit. "But if we can make Tigger feel Small and Sad just for **five minutes**, we shall have done a **good deed**."

So the only question was, where should they **lose Tigger**?

"We'll take him to the **North Pole**," said Rabbit.

"It was a long explore finding it, so it will be a very long explore for Tigger **un**-finding it again."

Pooh felt glad. It was he who had first found the North Pole so when they got there, Tigger would see a notice saying,

and Tigger would then know what sort of bear he was.

**That** sort of bear. So it was arranged that they would start the **next morning** and Rabbit would go and ask Tigger to come.

The next day was quite a different day. Instead of being sunny, it was **cold and misty**. Pooh felt sorry for the bees who wouldn't be making honey on such a day. Piglet wasn't thinking of that, but of how **cold and miserable** it would be being lost **all day and night** on top of the Forest on such a day.

Rabbit said it was just the day for them. As soon as Tigger bounced out of sight, they would hurry in the other direction, and he would never see them again.

"Not never?" said Piglet, worriedly.

"Well, not until we find him again," said Rabbit.

"Come on. He's waiting for us."

At Kanga's house, they found Roo waiting for them too.

This made things **Very Awkward.**

Rabbit whispered behind his paw to Pooh, "Leave

this to me!"

"Roo had better not come today," he said to Kanga.

"He was coughing earlier."

"Oh Roo, you never told me," said Kanga, reproachfully.

"It was a **biscuit cough,**" said Roo, "not one you

tell about."

"I think not today, dear. Another day," Kanga said.

"Ah, Tigger! There you are!" said Rabbit, happily.

"All ready? Come on."

So they went.

At first Pooh and Rabbit and
Piglet walked together, and
Tigger ran round them
in circles. Then, when the
path got narrower, Rabbit,
Piglet and Pooh walked one

after another, and Tigger ran round them in oblongs.

When the gorse got very
prickly, Tigger ran up
and down in front of
them, and sometimes
bounced into Rabbit.

As they got higher, the mist got thicker, so Tigger kept
disappearing, and then bouncing back again.

Rabbit nudged Piglet. "The next time," he said.
"Tell Pooh."
"The next what?" said Pooh.
Tigger appeared,
bounced into Rabbit
and disappeared again.

"Now!" said Rabbit. He jumped into a hollow and Pooh and Piglet jumped in after him.

The Forest was silent. They could see nothing and hear nothing.

Then they heard Tigger pattering about.

"Hallo?" he said.

Then they heard him pattering off again.

They waited a little longer and then Rabbit got up.

"Well!" he said proudly. "Just as I said! Come on, let's go!"

They all hurried off, with Rabbit leading the way.

"Why are we going along here?" said Pooh.

"Because it's the way home!" said Rabbit.

"I *think* it's more to the right," said Piglet, nervously.

They went on. "Here we are," said Rabbit, ten

minutes later. "No, we're not . . ."

"It's a funny thing," said Rabbit, another ten minutes later,

"how everything looks the same in a mist.

Lucky we know the Forest so well, or we might get lost."

Piglet sidled up to Pooh from behind.

"Pooh!" he whispered.

"Yes, Piglet?"

"Nothing," said Piglet, taking Pooh's paw. "I just wanted to

be sure of you."

When Tigger had finished waiting for the others to catch him up, and they hadn't, he decided he would go home. Kanga gave him a basket and sent him off with Roo to collect fir-cones.

Tigger and Roo threw pine cones at each other until they had quite forgotten what they came for. They left the basket under the trees and went back for dinner.

Just as they were finishing dinner, Christopher Robin put his head around the door and asked,

"Where's Pooh?"

Tigger explained what had happened and Christopher Robin realised Pooh, Piglet and Rabbit were lost in the mist on the top of the Forest. "It's a funny thing about Tiggers," Tigger whispered to Roo, "they never get lost." "Well," said Christopher Robin

to Tigger, "we shall have to go back and find them."

Rabbit, Pooh and Piglet were having a rest in a sand-pit.
Pooh was **rather tired** of the sand-pit, because whichever
direction they started in, they always ended up at it again.

"Well," said Rabbit after a while. "We'd better get on.
Which way shall we try?"

"How about we leave," said Pooh, "and as soon as we're out
of sight of the sand-pit, we try to find it again?"

"What's the good of that?" asked Rabbit.

"Well," said Pooh, "we keep looking for Home and not
finding it, so if we looked for this pit, we'd be sure not to
find it, and we might find **something** we *weren't* looking
for, which might be just what we were looking for **really.**"

"Try," said Piglet to Rabbit, suddenly. "We'll wait
here for you."

Rabbit walked into the mist.

After Pooh and Piglet had waited twenty minutes for him, Pooh got up.

"Let's go home, Piglet," he said. "There are twelve pots of honey in my cupboard, and they've been calling to me for hours. I couldn't hear them because Rabbit would talk, but if nobody is saying anything then I shall know where they are. Come on."

They walked off together. For a long time Piglet said nothing, then suddenly he made a squeaky noise because now he began to know where he was. Just when he was getting sure, there was a shout and out of the mist came Christopher Robin.

"Oh! There you are," said Christopher Robin

carelessly, trying to pretend he hadn't been anxious.

"Here we are," said Pooh.

"Where's Rabbit?" asked Christopher Robin.

"I don't know," said Pooh.

"Oh – well, I expect Tigger will find him. He's sort of

looking for you all," said Christopher Robin.

"Well," said Pooh, "I've got to go home for *something* and

so has Piglet, because we haven't had it yet, and –"

"I'll come and watch you," said Christopher Robin.

So he went home with Pooh and watched him for some time.

All the time Christopher Robin was watching Pooh, Tigger was tearing around the Forest making loud yapping noises for Rabbit. And at last, a very Small and Sorry Rabbit heard him. And the Small and Sorry Rabbit rushed through the mist at the noise, and it suddenly turned into Tigger:

a Friendly Tigger,

a Grand Tigger,

a Large and Helpful Tigger,

a Tigger who bounced, if he bounced at all, in just the beautiful way a Tigger ought to bounce.

"Oh Tigger, **I am glad** to see you," cried Rabbit.

# The End